It was that special time of year. Mrs. Jumbo, the elephant, searched the sky. If she was lucky, a stork would bring her a baby.

But she was unlucky again. "Now I'll have to wait until next year," she sighed as she boarded the circus train. The circus was moving to another town.

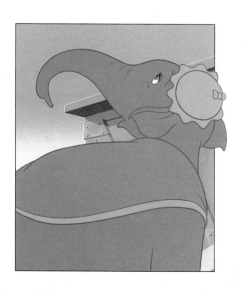

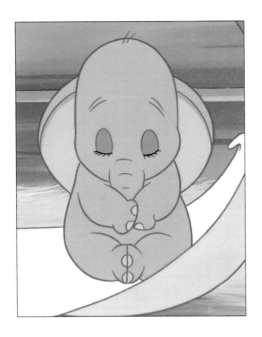

Mrs. Jumbo was standing in her train car when she heard a thump. She turned around to see a stork with a package. "Here is your baby. Sign here, please," he said.

Mrs. Jumbo untied the package. "He looks perfect," she said.

All the other elephants came to admire the
new baby elephant.

Then, the baby let out a sneeze that unfolded
his enormous ears. The other elephants said he
looked so silly he should be called Dumbo.
Mrs. Jumbo turned away from them, and
hugged her baby tight.

At the next town, the animals marched in a
big parade to announce the arrival of the
circus. Dumbo marched behind his mother.

After the parade, the animals went back to the
circus tents. Dumbo was eating dinner when a
boy appeared and started pulling at his ears.
"That's the funniest thing I ever saw!"
he yelled.

Dumbo let out a cry of fright, and his mother grabbed the mean boy with her trunk. She spanked him just enough to scare him.

But the boy told everyone that Mrs. Jumbo had gone wild, and had attacked him. So the trainers tied her up and locked her away.

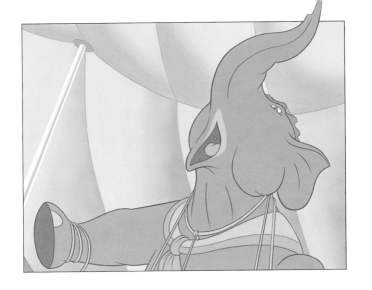

The other elephants would not help Dumbo find his mother. They thought everything was his fault.

Dumbo was all alone, crying, when Timothy Q. Mouse appeared. "I think you're great," he said, and promised to make Dumbo a star.

Timothy gave the Ringmaster an idea for Dumbo's act. He imagined Dumbo waving a little flag at the top of a pyramid of elephants.

At the next performance, the Ringmaster tried out his new act. Dumbo was scared when the spotlight shone on him, but then he ran into the ring. Suddenly, his ears came untied, he tripped over them, and went flying into the ball the elephants were balancing on. The tower of elephants came crashing down, and terrified the audience.

The Ringmaster came up with another new act for Dumbo. He had to dress up like a baby clown, and jump out of a pretend burning building into a tub of sticky cream. Everybody laughed, which made Dumbo feel like crying.

But later, Timothy told him where he could visit his mother. Mrs. Jumbo cradled him in her trunk through the bars of her cage.

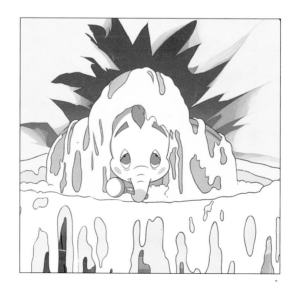

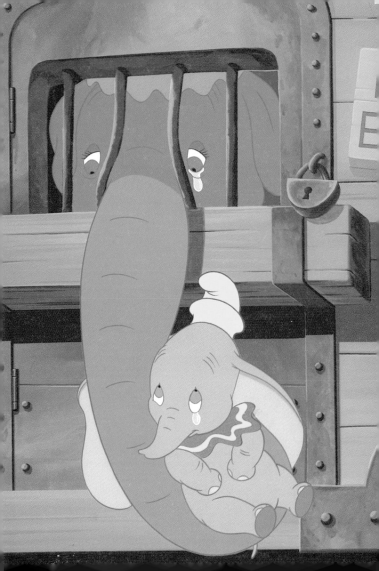

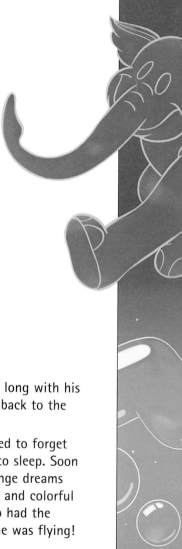

Dumbo could not stay long with his
mother. He had to go back to the
circus.

That night, Dumbo tried to forget
his problems and get to sleep. Soon
he began to have strange dreams
full of floating shapes and colorful
elephants. And Dumbo had the
weird sensation that he was flying!

The next morning, a group of crows found
Dumbo and Timothy sleeping in a tree. Their
chattering woke Dumbo up, and he fell off
the branch into a stream. The crows shrieked
with laughter.

Timothy was angry. "What's so funny about a
poor little elephant falling out of a tree?"
he demanded.

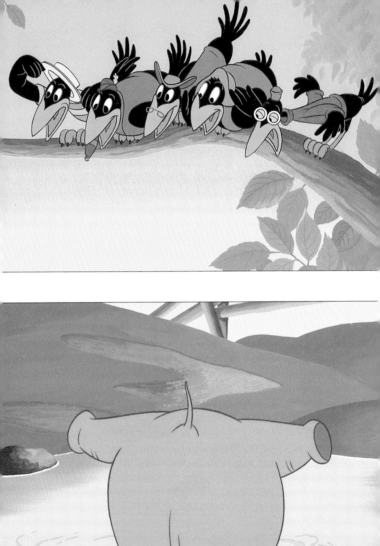

Then Timothy had a thought. "How did he get up into the tree?" he asked.

"Maybe he flew!" The crows cackled. This did not seem possible. But the crows gave Dumbo a feather, which they said was magic. Then they encouraged him to fly. Dumbo stood nervously and closed his eyes.

The crows gave Dumbo a shove, yelling "Heave ho — off you go!"

Believe it or not, Dumbo began to fly.

"I knew you could do it! Look! We're flying!" shouted Timothy, who was riding in Dumbo's hat.

Dumbo opened his eyes. It was true! He was flying like a bird, just like in his dream. Flying was wonderful!

That night, Dumbo had to jump again out
of the clowns' burning building. This time
he was not afraid. He had his magic feather.

But just as he jumped, he accidentally
dropped it. Then Timothy shouted, "That
feather isn't magic! You can fly if you
believe you can!"

And so he did!

Dumbo became an overnight sensation. Everywhere the circus went, people came to see Dumbo the Flying Elephant.

Dumbo performed nose dives and spins and loop-the-loops, and Mrs. Jumbo watched proudly from her place of honor. Dumbo was the star of the circus. Everyone loved him now!